THE
IGUANA
COOKBOOK

"SAVE FLORIDA"

EAT AN IGUANA

by George Cera

THANK you for coming
To BOCA Grande FL

George Cera

I would like to thank the people of Boca Grande for welcoming me into their community.

I would also like to thank Jong Bonaire for contributing one of the recipes in this book. Jong Bonaire is an after-school activity center for teenagers on the Caribbean island of Bonaire. In 2009, we celebrate 50 years of service to the Bonaire community and 10 years for our teen program. Please visit them at www.jongbonaire.org

PHOTO CREDITS
George Cera
Tim Litwiller
Kathi Rader-Gibson
Marcy Shortuse

PROOF READING
Marcy Shortuse

SHORT STORY
Jesse Cera
Marcy Shortuse

WRITTEN BY
George Cera
A full color edition of this book is also available at
iguanacookbook.com
TheIguanaHunter.com

COVER & BOOK DESIGN
Isabella Wasser
Macdesigner1127@aol.com

This book is dedicated to my children
Jesse and Marlana.

A special thanks to
Jade - The Iguana Supermodel
posing for the front cover.

I would also like to thank his roommates
Pat & Kat Chadwick.
Jade is a world traveler and loves to sail to tropical
locations with his roommates, where his favorite
past time is basking in the sun, drinking green tea
and nibbling on kale.

*"You don't have to tell me I am beautiful, I know I am,
but thanks anyway."*

One night, on an island surrounded by water and palm trees, a man contemplated the several caged iguanas before him in his backyard. He had collected the iguanas over the years for his grandson, but, as fate would have it, the child had to move away and left his pets behind.

The man looked around, realizing how close his island home's environment was to the native lands of the lizards. Slowly he reached down… turning the latch on the cage, opening the door. The lizards slipped out and disappeared into the shadows.

In just over 30 years time, that small group of iguanas would turn into approximately 12,000, and would take over the landscape of a once-sleepy island village, turning it into "The Island of the Iguana."

Thank you for buying this book.

I'm George M. Cera, some know me for my work in the town of Boca Grande, Florida as the Iguana Hunter, "Iguana guy" or just as "That Guy" that is getting the iguanas off the island.

The story I just told is, for all intents and purposes, true. A long-time island resident has, indeed, admitted to turning his grandson's pet iguanas loose over 30 years ago.

He also said, though, that he wasn't the only one to do

it, which leaves the question as to whether he was the true culprit that unleashed an iguana menace on the island.

I'll tell you more about my work later on in this book.

Oh, and by the way, I prefer to be called "George".

George's Story

A little about me, and maybe a little insight into my view of nature. As a boy I always had a great love for wildlife and could always be found out in the woods, lakes and hills of northeast Ohio looking for critters of all types. I found a sense of peace in the woods and fields, mixed with wonderment at all of the life and miniature dramas that I would witness happening all around me.

As a young boy I remember sitting and watching ants rebuild their ant hill after a summer rain wore it down. I remember thinking how small they were, and especially how amazing it was that they could rebuild the mound, so much bigger than them, with no tools. For us, it would compare to building the New York Subway System with our teeth!

I think I was about eight years old, and even then I remember thinking that humans undertake such massive building projects like dams, highways, sky scrapers ... and while sometimes it's for the unselfish betterment of humanity, more often than not it is for ego or greed. These ants were doing it for the benefit of the whole nest. No one ant felt more important than the other, and they didn't get an ant pat on the back to say "Hey, nice job". They were doing it for the safety and well-being of the whole colony. I remember thinking then that they were doing it because it was the right thing to do.

Maybe humans can learn from the lowly ants about doing the right thing.

These ants led me to want to learn all that I possibly could about animals and nature. How does it all work? Why do animals do what they do? How do all of the pieces fit to form a healthy, working ecosystem - for them and for US?

Through the years of my ongoing journey of under-standing, I have learned that there is NO SUCH THING AS A BAD ANIMAL! They just do what they do to survive.

Something To Think About

When humans start putting labels on wildlife like "GOOD" or "BAD" animals, especially to children, we opened the door to diluted, pre-conceived ideas that lead to US OR THE ANIMAL BEING HURT!

A good example of this is in kid's cartoons. Furry

animals such as raccoons, stray cats and dogs are portrayed as "good." When your children see one they think it's OK to touch them or feed them. This normally ends in a painful bite and a trip to the hospital for stitches. It also means that if the animal can't be found, rabies shots will be required. To top it off, mental and physical scars can be left behind on the young victim.

The same cartoons will portray snakes, sharks and spiders as demonic minions from hell who find no greater joy than inflicting pain and laying in wait to take one of us poor humans out. Because of this attitude many innocent animals are killed, maimed and tortured because they are perceived to be bad - It's just not true!

When you enter the woods, lakes, and oceans, try to

think of it the same way you would if you went to someone's home, or someone coming to yours.

There are rules. Don't tear things up, have respect for those living there and their things. If you do this, you are welcome back. If you don't, there will be some type of consequences for your behavior. Take the time to educate yourself and, more importantly, your children, to be safe and have respect and compassion for all living things. That said - get out there, have fun, enjoy, but don't feed or touch.

Please, treat all wildlife respectfully!

Snake Bite Trivia

The truth of the matter is that more than 90% of venomous snake bites in the United States happen when the bite victim is harassing or trying to handle the snake. IT'S ALWAYS BEST TO LEAVE THEM ALONE!

Don't get me wrong, I do understand phobias. I'm not telling anyone that they have to love or even like all animals, just don't be mean and let them have room to live.

To tell you the truth, for example, I hate ticks!! I don't go out of my way to hurt them, but I hate them. When I was 18, let's just say I had one of those little blood sucking b@!%@ attach himself, to, well, somewhere that was a little bit to intimate for my liking! I saw it and screamed like a school girl! Now, 22 years later, thinking of that moment I get a creepy crawly feeling inside! YUCK!

OK, that is a whole other story. Back to the point.

What Is An Iguana?

The word iguana is derived from a Spanish form of the Taino name for this animal - **Iwana**. The **Tainos** were the original inhabitants of the Bahamas and Antilles Islands.

The "Iwana" or iguana was first officially described as a species by Swedish botanist Carolus Linnaeus in 1758. In the two centuries since then, no less than 17 species of iguana have been identified. The iguana

Male Spiny Tailed Iguana

belongs to a family of lizards native to tropical areas of Central and South America and the Caribbean. The genus iguana includes two species: the green iguana and the lesser Antillean iguana.

Right now in Florida we are having problems with two species of iguana, **the black spiny-tailed iguana (otherwise known as the black iguana, or Ctenosaura similes) and the green iguana (otherwise known as Iguana iguana).**

The black spiny-tailed iguana or black iguana is native to Mexico and Central America and has been introduced to Florida. It is the largest species of the genus Ctenosaura with males getting up to 50 inches long and females slightly smaller. This animal is extremely fleet of foot. The *Guinness Book of World Records* lists the running speed of this species at 21.7 miles per hour (35 km per hour), making it the fastest lizard on earth.

The black spiny-tailed iguana was first described by British zoologist John Edward Gray in 1831. The generic name **Ctenosaura** is derived from two Greek words "cteno" meaning "comb" (referring to the comb like spines on the lizard's back and tail) and "saura" meaning "lizard."

I have worked in the field with black spiny-tailed iguana for two years in Boca Grande. During that time I removed 16,000 iguanas from the island and I can

attest to the fact that they are fast, agile, adaptable and intelligent animals. They have come close to wiping out any of the island's smaller animals that they could fit into their mouths.

The green iguana is a reptile commonly found in captivity as a pet and grows up to 1.5 meters in length from head to tail, although a few specimens have grown more than 2 meters (6 feet) and can weigh upwards of 20 lbs (10 kg).

Florida's Iguana Problem

Green iguanas are considered an invasive species in South Florida and along the Gulf Coast of Florida from Key West to Pinellas County. This is due to a combination of events. The original small iguana populations in

Wild green iguana basking on the sidewalk
Siesta Key, Florida

the Florida Keys were animals that had arrived as stowaways on ships that carried fruit from South America. It is also thought that some may have arrived by rafting on

Notice the claws on this green iguana that it uses for climbing and self defense.

vegetation that was blown into the Florida Keys by hurricanes and storms.

To make matters worse, many iguanas have escaped or were intentionally released from the pet trade. They survived and then thrived in their new habitat.

Today, iguana numbers in Florida are possibly reaching into the millions. They are commonly found hiding in attics, under houses and on the beaches. They often destroy gardens, landscaping and native Floridian plants, which in turn displaces indigenous wildlife.

Two endangered plants they seem to be fond of eating are **Cordia Globosa** and **Nicker nut (Caesalpinia)**. Nicker nut is the primary food plant of the endangered Miami Blue Butterfly **(Cyclargus thomasi bethunebakeri)**. Additionally, on Marco Island, green iguanas have been observed using the burrows of the Florida burrowing owl, a species of special concern.

Florida burrowing owl, besides being displaced from their burrows by the green iguana. Chicks and eggs are also fed upon by the black spiny tailed iguana.

All of these factors make iguanas more of a serious threat to Florida's ecosystem than anyone originally believed.

A Video That Caught My Attention

I saw a video on the internet called "Blood Thirsty Iguana" that I thought captured a very interesting behavior.

The video was taken of a group of people in the tropics, probably on vacation. They were sitting and chatting on their porch when an iguana came up to them looking for a handout. As they are chatting, talking about their new reptilian friend, the iguana walked up to them and nipped at a guy's toes.

In the video it really didn't look like much of a bite. After a moment, though, you could see small droplets of blood on the floor as he started walking.

OK, so you're thinking - George, get to the point!

What I found to be amazing was that the iguana was following the guy, licking up the tiny puddles of blood! Why did this get my attention you might ask? Because it didn't appear to me that the iguana was exploring a new taste sensation ... he knew what it was and he liked it.

The footage from that video leads me to believe that the iguana knew that blood was animal protein, making me think it had definitely fed on some smaller, weaker animal in the past.

The iguana in that video had obviously been fed by people before. In reality, I have never seen iguanas come up to humans, except in areas where tourists and locals had been feeding them. When the group of people in the video didn't feed that iguana, he became more excited and persistent and nipped at their toes. So you know what that means - the next time you see a sign that says "DON'T FEED THE ANIMALS," you'll know why.

With that video fresh in my mind, later in the day I was making dinner for my kids. As I was preparing some lamb with Willis, our cat, rubbing in a figure-eight fashion between my legs and meowing and begging for scraps, I thought I would experiment a little bit.

My question was, do all green iguanas like meat? Or did the iguana in the video become accustomed to it from getting it in the way of hand-outs from tourists?

I had an idea.

Being an "outdoorsy iguana" kind of guy, I just so happened to have an iguana laying around the house, sleeping on top of the TV in the living room to be precise. Rusty is his name, he's about a four-footer (I will be telling much more about him later).

Back to the story.

I cut a strip of lean meat off of the leg of lamb and offered it to Rusty. He was sleeping at the time, so I touched that piece of meat to his face, but he didn't want

Willis and Rusty jostling for the best spot on the couch.

to wake up. Then he slowly flicked his tongue and took a taste of this thing that was bothering his rest.

To my surprise, his eyes flew open and he greedily gobbled down the lamb meat.

Then, to my absolute horror, he jumped down from atop the TV and ate the cat!

I'm joking, settle down, he really didn't eat our cat. He didn't even try to give the cat a little taste.

What Rusty the iguana and Willis the cat *did* do was follow me out to the kitchen to try to beg for more lamb. Needless to say the two of them lost out. Willis the cat because the roast was already in the oven and Rusty because I put my shoes on.

Now don't get too alarmed thinking you have to worry about a new type of half-vampire, half-iguana mutant sneaking in at night to suck the blood from the toes of you children.

But, unfortunately, Florida's plants, birds and small animals in an iguana's eyes are "What's for dinner tonight?"!

My Work In Boca Grande, Florida

Gasparilla Island is located on the west coast of Florida. It is one of Charlotte Harbor's Barrier Islands, located about 50 miles south of Sarasota. It is a smaller island, eight miles long and a half mile wide, split between a mile-long portion in Charlotte County and a seven-mile stretch within Lee County. Gasparilla Island has a rich and colorful history, dating back to 500 BC with the Calusa Indians, which were the dominant tribe of the region and inhabitants of the island. The fictitious pirate Jose Gaspar, after whom the island was named, supposedly made Charlotte Harbor his home base in 1783.

Then in 2005, the people of Boca Grande formed the Boca Grande "iguana tax" panel to deal with the ongoing iguana problem to determine how, when and why iguanas on the island would be exterminated.

The rest of that story will be in my next book, but for right now the only thing I can say is, "You had to be there." It was an interesting, comical ride.

Boca Grande is the name of the only village on the island, located on the Lee County side. This island is know worldwide for it's tarpon fishing and a place where old world Florida meets the "Who's Who" of the rich and famous. Now it is also known for its iguanas and for giving birth to me - Florida's original "Iguana Hunter!"

In November of 2006 I became to be a part of the island's history, when I was awarded the contract to catch iguanas for the Lee County portion of the island. During the months of November, December and January I really wasn't able to do much iguana-catching because the weather was too cold at night and the iguanas weren't very active. Instead, what I was doing during that time was scouting the island, looking for iguana guano (poo), tracks and signs of iguana activity.

The Lee County side of the island has a lot of protected land. These tracts of land are protected for the native plants and animals.

After two weeks of scouting I noticed a very disturbing trend! There were very few small, native animals to be found. In some areas, there were none.

While I wasn't seeing small birds, snakes, anole (American chameleon), small gopher tortoises or even fiddler crabs, I was seeing iguana signs everywhere. From tracks in the sand, to guano containing bird feathers, egg shells, snail shells and hair, I knew something bad was going on and it was really bothering me.

So I hit the books and internet looking for information on the habits of the black spiny-tailed iguana.

Female black spiny tailed iguana raiding Downey woodpecker nest.

The information that I read said that **Ctenosaura** were omnivores as juveniles, eating both plants and animals, but became herbivores (vegetarians) as adults.

I found out that this is not the case.

As the weather warmed up and iguanas became more active, I saw them everywhere, catching and eating anything that would fit into their mouths. I want you to keep in mind that we're talking about an animal that can run at speeds over 20 miles and hour, can jump and climb a tree as easily as it is for us to walk through our kitchen, can grow up to 50 inches long and, pound for pound, has the bite force of an alligator.

A large male black spiny-tailed iguana gobbles up a juvenile gopher tortoise like we would a cherry tomato.

Male black spiny tailed iguanas in a territorial battle.

The native animals in Boca Grande could not compete with such an agile, intruding predator ... and the native wildlife was in a state of decline.

The population of iguanas on the island was at such a high level that I would see iguanas regularly feeding on each other.

Other observations I made were that iguanas were climbing into garbage cans, scavenging food. They are also very good hunters and won't hesitate running down their prey in the same fashion as a cat.

Watching the hunt was amazing. I've seen them dive out of trees and grab birds, squirrels and snakes.

I have seen firsthand the damage done by iguanas introduced into Florida's ecosystem. There is a battle for life happening in the backyards of Florida, and our native animals are losing the fight.

What We Are Going To Lose

Gopher tortoise (gopherus polyphemus)

The Gopher tortoise is a great example. Listed as an "animal of concern" (meaning that they are protected by law), their importance to Florida's natural environment is immeasurable. As their name suggests, the tortoises will excavate many burrows in their home territory which they use at different times for shelter from the elements or to escape predators.

There are also 300 species of animals in Florida that use the unoccupied burrows that the tortoise will dig.

Black spiny tailed iguana bullying gopher tortoise trying to take over its burrow.

Some of these animals are **solely** dependent on gopher tortoises and their burrows for their survival.

When the iguanas established themselves on the island, they started using the burrows instead. They would also feed on the eggs and young tortoises or any other occupants that were found in the burrows that were unable to fight back.

Knowing this information, and that there are so many other species dependent on the gopher tortoise, the domino effect has the potential of wiping out 300 species of animals.

Now you can see why I feel that the stage is set for an ecological disaster and species extinction. If put on a human scale, it would be the equivalent to a nuclear bomb blast in a major city.

This is not an exaggeration. Remember, I do have years of experience with iguanas and two years comprised of 4,000 hours working with and observing the black spiny-tailed iguana in the field. My concerns are based on what I have witnessed.

Life With Rusty, The Iguana

I mentioned Rusty the iguana earlier in this book, and here is his story.

In September of 2007 I was working on my project in Boca Grande and got a call from The Wildlife Center of Venice (a wildlife sanctuary and hospital about 30 miles north of

Rusty getting his beauty sleep on the top of the TV

Gasparilla), telling me that someone had brought them a green iguana that had been caught wandering in their yard, and now they weren't sure what to do. I told them I would come take a look at him later that evening.

When I arrived at the center, the first thing that I noticed about this iguana was his color, a bright rusty orange. He was well over three feet long and very docile. I noticed that someone had painted the word "iguana" in big letters with purple fingernail polish on both his sides (sometimes people make me sick).

As I looked at him through the chicken wire of his holding cage I could tell that he has had a tough go at life up to this point.

Now the question was, what to do with him? I truly believe that iguanas are not good pets. They have very specific nutritional needs and the males are known for aggressive behavior during breeding season. They don't care who you are or how big you are ... if so inclined, they will attack!

As I was looking at him thinking the best thing would be to euthanize him, he lifted his head and looked at me with a tired, defeated stare, then laid his head down and closed his eyes.

I honestly don't know what it was about that moment or that particular iguana, but I said to myself, "Darn it! I will take you and give you the best life I can!"

I took my new reptilian friend home that night and then straight to the vet the next day, to see Dr. Jack Landis at the Nokomis Veterinary Clinic. Dr. Landis took blood samples and x-rays of Rusty. Just as I suspected, he was in bad health because of inadequate care and poor diet administered by his previous own-ers. Rusty's x-rays showed that he had several joints in his right hind leg that were malformed and that he had a rock hard, golfball-sized deposit of uric acid in his bladder that would have to be surgically removed.

Rusty posing for his photo interview for the Boca Beacon newspaper.

Now yet again I'm thinking - do I keep him or have him put to sleep? To make a long story short, I asked Dr. Landis, who is very well known and respected for his work with reptiles, if he thought Rusty was in pain because of the dam-aged joints in his leg. His answer to me was he didn't believe that it was painful to Rusty. With that in mind I told Dr. Landis to go ahead and operate. The operation was a complete success and Rusty made a full recovery.

A month or so went by and Rusty became a regular part of the family. He gets up in the morning and I take him outside to go to the bathroom, then he comes back into the house for his breakfast of assorted fruits, leafy greens, and veggies sprinkled with a dash of vitamin powder. After breakfast he's off to the business of harassing Willis the cat. Once Willis is sufficiently annoyed, Rusty heads off to his favorite couch to bask in the sun and rapidly nod his head at anyone watching him, asserting his rule over his kingdom. For the most part, that was a day with Rusty.

That is, unless it's iguana breeding season!

This is the part of the story where everyone, especially those who think they want an iguana as a pet, should take note.

It was mid January and Marlana, my daughter, and I were sitting watching TV in the living room. She was on one end of the couch and Rusty and I were on the other. Rusty was in his spot on the back of the couch and it was life as normal. As Marlana and I were chatting about life, out of the blue Rusty let out a "hiss." I turned to see what he was fussing about.

What I saw was Rusty with his mouth wide open and his pupils constricted in rage. Just as I turned and saw the menacing sight, the little creep lunged at me, trying to bite me in the face! As he jumped off the couch I grabbed him, trying to stop his attack! Marlana was screaming as I was trying to get control of Rusty, the 4.5 foot buzz saw. As he was whipping me with his tail and digging his claws into my hands and arms, trying to get into position to inflict a good bite, I was able to roll over the back of the couch and lock him in the bathroom, stopping his unprovoked attack.

With the homicidal iguana locked safely in the bathroom and me standing there battered and bloody, my 17-year-old daughter was flipping right out about what she just witnessed. I was trying to tend to my wounds and explain to Marlana that Rusty's hormones were going nuts because of iguana breeding season.

Marlana didn't want to hear it, she said there was no excuse for his behavior and told me I should get rid of him.

"No Marlana, being a woman you know that hormones can make you feel and do some pretty irrational things," I said.

All I was trying to do was explain to her that Rusty's hormones were much like hers would be at her "time of the month."

It was the wrong thing to say.

Now, not only did I have an irate hormonal iguana locked up in the bathroom, I now had a thoroughly irate, hormonal teenage daughter letting me know that my statement about women getting a little irrational at certain times was wrong and chauvinistic.

(Note to self - this is not something I should point out to ANY woman! Especially if I want to live!)

After about an hour everyone calmed down and I decided that Rusty was going to have to be in a cage until breeding season was over.

Later that day my 16-year-old son Jesse, who was absent for the iguana drama of the day, came home with one of this buddies. Seeing Rusty locked up, Jesse asked his sister why.

I was in the kitchen doing the dishes and could hear Marlana telling Jesse about Rusty's outburst and bad behavior, and the epic battle that ensued. I could hear her telling them how I fell over the back of the couch trying to get Rusty under control and the three of them giggled.

My ego was shattered. I felt that it was a perfectly executed move even Jackie Chan would have been proud to perform. The way my daughter told it, I looked more like a drunken sailor tripping over his sea bag.

The teenage boys were cracking up to hear about the five pound iguana that darn near beat up the 275 lb "Iguana Hunter." (Real funny guys!)

I was still in the kitchen when I heard my son yell to me that he was going to get Rusty out of the cage. "That is not a good idea," I told him.

Anyone that remembers being a teenage boy or knows one also knows that they do not listen. OH NO!

I came around the corner of the living room to see Jesse sitting on the couch with Rusty, kissing him on his head, showing off for his friend who was busy taking a picture with his cell phone.

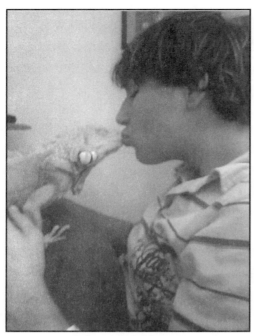

I said it again. "Jesse, I'm telling you, you're going to get hurt, put him back!"

Jesse sat Rusty down across his lap and said "Dad, you must have done something to make him mad, he's not going to hurt me."

That fateful kiss.
Yes, this is the real picture.

Jesse had no sooner said those words, when Rusty bit down on Jesse's forearm and was clamping down with everything he had. Jesse let out a blood-curdling scream of pain "AAAAHHH, you little @#$%! AAHHHH, Dad! Get him off! AHHH!!! Get him OFF ME!!!"

As I watched, my son was jumping around our living room like his feet were on fire and his butt was catching, all with Rusty dangling from his arm. It was total chaos.

I ran over and grabbed Jesse's arm, then I grabbed Rusty.

"Jesse, I know this really hurts, but I can't yank him off of you," I said. "If I do, you are going to loose that hunk of skin!"

I explained that I would have to flip Rusty over to his back, at which point he would let go. We did and Rusty let go.

More out of shock than anything, Jesse's friend and I started laughing. I waited for a few minutes before rubbing it in.

"So what did you do to make him mad?" I asked.

Here's another story about Rusty's antics. I'll have my son Jesse tell you. It's pretty funny now, but it wasn't when it happened!

Hi, my name is Jesse Cera. The story I am about to tell you is one about our 4 foot iguana named Rusty and my princess minded 17 year old sister Marlana. This is an image I will remember for the rest of my life.

My sister is in no way an animal lover, so Rusty is not well-liked either, as far as that is concerned.

As I was getting ready to leave my house one morning with my friend Mike to go spear fishing in Boca Grande, Marlana asked me to put Rusty in his cage before I left. I didn't want him to be locked up all day, so I agreed to it, but never did put him in his cage. Mike and I left after that. We got about 20 minutes down the road when I got a frantic phone call! All I could make out was horrified screaming and "He's chasing me! I'm on the table! Help!"

Now, knowing my sister, I assumed she was just being dramatic as a payback for me not listening to her. I did, of course, offer my immediate assistance by simply saying, "Marlana, he weighs five pounds, just don't look at him! He will leave you alone."

And with that I hung up the phone.

She didn't call back, so I thought everything was fine. About another 20 minutes went by when my dad called and asked me if I talked to Marlana. I said that I did and I thought she was lying to me about what was going on. Hearing that, my Pops was not happy and he demanded that I go home and help my sister because he was an hour away from home.

According to my dad, Marlana spent the last twenty minutes in a full-blown panic attack on the phone with him, waiting for me to come to her rescue.

So Mike and I turned around to go back to my house and help my sister.

Upon my arrival, I could only guess there must have been some sort of a struggle because my house was a mess. All the kitchen chairs were flipped over and as we came around the corner we saw Rusty standing on his hind legs, trying to get to Marlana who actually was on the kitchen table screaming! We lost it, we were laughing so hard! I hit the ground laughing so hard that I was on the brink of tears.

So, to save the day I went over and simply scooped Rusty up and set him back on his hot rock and the crisis was defused.

Once again, Jesse saved the day for his not-so-bright but still lovable sister."

I could go on and on about life with Rusty, but I'm going to wrap it up here.

Hopefully in this story you can see why I don't feel that iguanas make good pets. I have worked with them for a long time and know what to expect, and I was still caught off guard and could have been seriously hurt. People go to pet stores and see cute little baby iguanas and get them as pets, which then grow up and can become "too much work", or get aggressive and they are let go. So please, before you get an iguana or any other animal as a pet, learn about them first so you know how to care for them properly, their needs and lifespan and if they become aggressive as adults.

I really hope that you enjoyed what you have read. I wanted to keep it lightly informative and easy to read. So many times writers will get so wrapped up in their stories that it becomes mind-numbing. All the information we get bombarded with makes it easy to lose interest or the meaning of the story.

My goal is to try to educate and entertain my readers with facts and personal observations of a very real problem that Florida's native wildlife is facing. I don't claim to have all the answers to the problems. What I do know for sure is that if more work and effort isn't put into controlling the iguana problem, especially the black spiny-tails, we are going to lose many amazing, indigenous animals.

Before I start getting hate mail saying things like, **"How could you do that to a poor iguana?"** or **"Just leave them alone, they were here first?"** I need to explain.

I truly love and have respect for all animals, and all have their place and purpose and beauty. Unfortunately, iguanas don't belong in Florida. For every one iguana I get I'm saving hundreds, if not thousands of native animals. So instead of asking me, "How could I," especially if you have read the rest of this book, you need to be asking yourself what you can do to help.

When people tell me "The iguanas were here first," it really gets to me. Iguanas ARE NOT native to Florida. This is a manmade problem, WE brought them here, WE did it. Now that the damage is done, we need to be good stewards of nature and fix it.

Eating Iguanas

While some people may think iguanas are nasty creatures some cultures of the world think they are quite tasty.

Iguanas have been eaten for thousands of years. Green iguanas are nicknamed "Gallinas de Palo," which means "Tree Chicken". They are caught or raised for their meat. The taste and consistency of the cooked iguana is said to be similar to chicken, hence the nickname.

Iguana is eaten throughout Latin America, primarily in rural areas, and is usually grilled. The meat of the iguana is known to have a rich flavor because it feeds on jungle fruit. It is especially fond of papaya, giving the meat a tender texture and sweet flavor.

Many people also consider iguana meat an aphrodisiac, and it is also made into soup that is believed to be an old home remedy, like chicken soup, for strengthening those who are sick.

Here's another interesting bit of trivia about iguanas. Iguana was also declared a type of fish by the Catholic church, which made it OK to eat on meatless holidays.

OK, now you know iguanas have been a food source for people for thousands of years and that they are a remedy for the sick. God, through the wisdom of the Catholic Church, said that it is OK to eat iguanas anytime you want. *And ladies, if* your sweety tells you he has an iguana in his pants, he may not be lying. They are also said to an aphrodisiac.

So what's the problem? Get out there and do your part to save Florida! EAT AN IGUANA! Hehehe.

If I have convinced you to try it, you might be wondering how to find one. If you live in south Florida you can more than likely find one right in your own backyard, but the method you use to get one is up to you to decide. Just don't be cruel or BRAKE ANY LAWS, and don't risk your safety. I've met a lot of gardeners and landscape maintenance workers that will remove them from their customer's yards. Talk with them and see if they will get you an iguana.

Do not buy an iguana for meat from any source that catches the lizards outside the USA, PLEASE. The practice leads to poaching and will further threaten the iguana population in their home range.

Now that you have made it this far and you have your iguana, skin and clean the iguana in the same way that you skin and clean a chicken.

Remove the head, organs and tail. Then simply dip it in hot water and scrape the scales off the lizard as you would do with a fish. Remember to use all of the same safe food handling practices that you would when handling raw poultry. Iguanas do carry salmonella.

George's typical afternoon hunting iguanas on Sanibel Island

Thinking About Really Eating One?

Smells good! What's cooking?

Don't look at it as this bizarre, mystical meat. Think of it as a freaky-looking chicken.

Any way that you have ever cooked chicken, you can cook your "freaky chicken," whether it's barbecued, roasted, grilled, deep-fried, stir-fried, baked or in a soup.

However you cook it, just have fun exploring, enjoy and remember, if you got your "freaky chicken" out of your own backyard, you are doing your part to save Florida.

The following are some recipes to get you started on your ecologically friendly culinary journey.
Bon Appetite!

Simple Iguana

Cook the iguana in hot water until the meat softens a little. At this point you can add vegetables and spices according to whatever recipe you want to make and continue to cook the iguana in the boiling water. Alternatively, you can cook the iguana on a grill or in a pan until it browns on the outside and has a cooked and even consistency on the inside.

While the Iguana is cooking, think about fixing yourself one of these drinks ...

Green Iguana Margarita
    1 oz   Midori Melon Liqueur
    2 oz   Tequila (Two Fingers)
    4 oz   Sweet and Sour Mix

Blend and pour into a Margarita glass with salted rim. Makes 2 servings.

Iguana Sunrise Fizz
    1 oz   Tequila
    1 splash   7-Up soda
    3/4 oz   Triple Sec
    1/2 oz   Vodka
    1 3/4 oz   Orange Juice
    1 3/4 oz   Sweet and Sour Mix
Blend and serve over ice.

Iguana Juice
    1/2 oz   Vodka
    1/2 oz   Tequila
    1/4 oz   Coffee Liqueur
  1 1/2 oz   Sweet and Sour
            Slice of Lime

Naked Iguana
            Midori
            Orange Juice
            Grenadine

Sleeping Lizard Margaritas
    2 oz   Tequila
    2 oz   Sour Mix
    2 oz   Melon Liqueur
    1 oz   Lime Juice

Pink Banana
    1 oz   Creme de Banana
    5 oz   Pink Lemonade

Flying Pink Iguana
    1 oz   Vodka
    1 oz   Amaretto
            Pink Lemonade

Now that you've relaxed with a drink and are more prepared for the culinary world of the iguana, here are some more complicated recipes to try.

Iguana Burritos

1 lb	ground meat (iguana, chicken of beef)
1 tsp	chopped parsley
1	large onion, chopped
1	tsp tomato paste
1	clove garlic, pressed
1 tsp	Worcestershire sauce
1 tsp	salt
1/8 tsp	sugar
1 tsp	vinegar
3 or 4	capers

Cook until dry, wrap in tortilla or serve over nacho chips with favorite toppings. (Yummy)

Iguana and Rice

1	iguana or chicken, cut into pieces
3	cloves garlic (less if preferred)
1	sweet pepper
2	onions, chopped
1	tomato
1 1/2	cups of rice
3	cups of water saffron or bijol

Fry chopped onions, sweet pepper, tomato and garlic in a little bit of oil. Add water, saffron/bijol, iguana or chicken and washed rice. Cover and cook over a low flame until done, stirring once or twice during cooking. Will take approximately 50 to 60 minutes - make sure iguana or chicken and rice are well done.

Iguana Tacos

1	iguana
1	large onion
2	cloves garlic
3	tomatoes
2	green peppers
4 tsp	artichoke oil
1	pinch black pepper
	salt to taste

Make the artichoke oil by frying an artichoke slowly until the oil is red.

1. Cut off the iguanas head.

2. Open the belly lengthwise and remove all the entrails and the rectum.

3. Cook in salted water until the meat is tender (take care not to let it get too soft).

4. Peel and cut in portions.

5. Season with all the above ingredients and cook with about 1 cup water until almost dry.
Makes 4 servings.
Recipe By: Diana D. DePeralta

Creole Iguana

5	slices bacon
1 Tbsp	oil
5	drops sesame oil
2	celery stalks (chopped)
4	garlic cloves (minced)
1	cup water
1	cube chicken bouillon
	salt and pepper to taste
1 tsp	garlic powder
1 lb	iguana meat, bite-size pieces

Separately

3	medium tomatoes (diced)
1	garlic clove (minced)
1/2 tsp	salt
1 Tbsp	lime juice
1 1/2 Tbsp	chipotle flavored Tabasco sauce
1/2 tsp	chipotle chili pepper
	cilantro for garnish

Have your market vendor skin the iguana. The largest pieces of meat will be found on the legs and tail. Saute chopped bacon in both oils for 3 to 4 minutes. Add celery and garlic, stir and cook for 3 to 4 minutes more. Add water, chicken cube, salt, pepper and garlic powder. Stir well. Add iguana meat, cover and cook on low for 15 to 20 minutes. In a separate bowl, combine tomatoes, garlic, salt, lime juice and Tabasco. Mix well, then add to iguana. Add chili pepper and cook for 10 minutes. Serve over cooked rice, garnish with chopped cilantro. **Lots of cold cervezas on the side, of course!**

Yes, iguana does taste like chicken! According to Boì, a former chef at one of Bonaireís hotels, the main use of iguana is for "sÚpi di yuana" or iguana soup. It tastes just like chicken soup and the meat is very soft and tender. However, if you use a very large, old iguana it will be like using a large, old chicken - it will be tough.

Iguana for strength

Locals also believe that sÚpi di yuana and "yuana stob·" (iguana stew) are good for your health. They encourage sick or old people to eat it to get stronger. There is also the belief that if a man eats a lot of iguana he will have "hopi forsa" or much strength.

Contrary to what many people believe, iguana is not an endangered species and "sÚpi di yuana" is a traditional food for special occasions on Bonaire.

Cooking it

You can cook the iguana with or without the skin, but if you leave the skin on, you must clean the iguana like you would clean either a chicken and a fish. Dip it in hot water like you would to remove the feathers from a chicken, then scrape it to remove the scales, as you would a fish. Maybe this is why Boì prefers it without the skin. He says it tastes better, too.

BoÌ's recipe

1	iguana (at least two feet - 60 cm)
1 can	whole Italian tomatoes
1	large onion, chopped
3	stalks of celery, chopped
3 Tbsp	Yerba Hole, chopped (You can substitute basil for Yerba Hole which is a local herb)
3	medium potatoes, diced
2 cups	of iguana stock (or substitute chicken or turkey stock)

About 6 oz (200 gm) fine noodles

Salt and pepper to taste

Preparation:

First, catch your iguana! This can be done with a long pole with a noose at the end or, if you are quick enough, with your hands. Next, clean it well (see above). Cut the iguana into pieces about two inches (5 cm) long. Put the iguana in a large pot, cover well with water and simmer for about one hour or until the meat becomes soft. Skim the surface several times. Add tomato, onion, yerba hole, celery, noodles and stock. Simmer until the vegetables and noodles begin to soften. Add the potatoes and cook another ten minutes. Add salt and pepper to taste. Serve hot with bread, crackers or funchi (cornmeal pudding).

Bon appetite! © Jong Bonaire 2001

Iguana Pozole

2	medium iguanas
5 cups	freshly bleached hominy
10	cloves of garlic
1	onion
1	slice of cabbage - diced
	bay leaf
	Mexican oregano
	salt and pepper

Butcher skin and cut the iguana in pieces. Wash, salt and blanch for 15-20 minutes. Simmer the corn, garlic, onion, a bay leaf, and salt to taste. At 10 minutes add the meat. Cook for another 15-20 minutes. Serve with sliced cabbage, some of the onion slice, cilantro, oregano and pepper to taste.

Iguana roasted with Birria Marinade

1	medium iguana
8	guajillo chile
2	pasilla chile
4	cloves garlic
	oregano
	vinegar, salt pepper to taste

Butcher, skin and cut the iguana into pieces. Wash, salt and blanch for 15-20 minutes. Toast and soak the peppers. Blend the soaked chile with vinegar, oregano, salt and pepper to taste. Marinate the iguana meat in the mixture for at least two hours. Roast the iguana at high heat (450 degrees F) until tender.

Simple Curried Iguana

2 tsp	vegetable oil
1	onion, chopped
1	green or red bell pepper, diced
1	clove garlic, chopped fine
1 1/2	Tbsp curry powder
1/2 tsp	dried thyme
1 lb	canned, chopped tomatoes
2 Tbsp	lemon juice
1/2 cup	water
2 oz	currants or raisins
	salt and pepper
3 lbs	iguana, skinned and cut into pieces
	cooked rice to serve

Preheat oven to 350 degrees. Heat oil in frying pan, add onion, pepper and garlic. Cook until soft. Stir in curry powder, thyme, tomatoes, lemon juice and water. Bring to boil. Add currants or raisins and season to taste. Put iguana pieces in the pan, coating with sauce. Cover and cook about 40 minutes or until tender in oven. Serve with rice.

Iguana and Vegetable Ball Soup

1 1/2 to 2	cups chopped, cooked iguana
2	bamboo shoots, cut into very thin strips
4	mushrooms, chopped
2	small carrots, finely chopped
1	egg, beaten
1/2	cup plus 1 tsp soy sauce
4	tsp sugar
3	cups chicken stock

Combine iguana, bamboo shoots, mushrooms, carrots, egg, 1 tsp soy sauce and 1 tsp sugar. Mix well and form into balls.

Place chicken stock, 1/2 cup soy sauce and remaining 1 Tbsp sugar in large saucepan. Bring to a boil. Drop iguana balls into boiling stock, reduce heat and simmer for 8 minutes and serve.

Iguana Stew

3 to 4 lbs	iguana
	Boiling water
1 tsp	salt
3	potatoes, peeled and sliced
1	large onion, sliced
1 cup	green lima beans
1 cup	canned tomatoes, sliced
1 Tbsp	sugar
1 cup	frozen corn
	Black pepper to taste
1 Tbsp	ketchup or Worcestershire sauce
1/4 cup	butter

Place iguana in Dutch oven with enough boiling water to cover. Add salt and simmer for 45 minutes.

Add potatoes, onion, lima beans, tomatoes and sugar to iguana. Cover and simmer for 30 minutes, or until beans and potatoes are tender.

Add corn, cover and simmer for 10 minutes. Season and add ketchup or Worcestershire sauce if desired. Add butter and stir well. Transfer to serving dish and serve hot.

Boiled Iguana with Mushroom Sauce

3	Tbsp vegetable oil
2	onions, chopped
2-3	stalks celery, chopped
4 lbs	iguana, cut into serving pieces
1	thick slice bacon, cut into pieces
	salt to taste
4	peppercorns
1	bay leaf
2 Tbsp	margarine
2 cups	sliced mushrooms
1 tsp	Worcestershire sauce
3 Tbsp	flour

Heat oil in large saucepan. Add onions and celery, saute for 3 to 4 minutes. Add iguana pieces and bacon. Add water to cover, salt, peppercorns and bay leaf. Bring to a boil, cover and simmer about 2 hours or until iguana is tender. Transfer iguana to a serving dish and keep warm. Strain and measure out 1 1/2 cups iguana broth.

Melt margarine in saucepan. Add mushrooms and saute 3 minutes. Stir in Worcestershire sauce and flour. Remove from heat and gradually add reserved iguana broth. Return to heat and whisk until boiling. Boil 2 minutes. Adjust seasoning and remove bay leaf. Pour sauce over iguana pieces and serve.

Thai Iguana Soup

1	Tbsp vegetable oil
1	garlic glove, finely chopped
1 lb	iguana meat skinned and chopped
1/2	tsp ground turmeric
1/4	tsp hot chili powder
3	ounces creamed coconut
3 3/4	cups hot chicken stock
2	Tbsp lemon or lime juice
2	Tbsp crunchy peanut butter
1 cup	threaded egg noodles, broken into small pieces
1	Tbsp scallions, finely chopped
1	Tbsp finely chopped fresh cilantro
	salt and black pepper
2	Tbsp dried coconut and 1/2 fresh red chili, seeded and finely chopped to garnish

Heat the oil in a large pan and fry the garlic for 1
minute until lightly golden. Add the iguana and spices
and fry for another 3- 6 minutes.
Crumble the creamed coconut into the hot chicken stock
and stir until dissolved. Pour onto the chicken and add
the lemon or lime juice, peanut butter and egg noodles.
Cover the pan and simmer for about 15 minutes,
Add the chopped scallions and cilantro, then season
well and cook for another 5 minutes. Meanwhile, place
the dried coconut oil in a small frying pan and heat for
2-3 minutes, stirring frequently.
Serve the soup in bowls and sprinkle each one with

some fried coconut and hot chili.
This filling and tasty soup Is very quick to prepare and cook.

Smoked Iguana Pizza

4	small pizza crusts, about 5 inches diameter
3	Tbsp olive oil
4	Tbsp sun-dried tomato paste
2	yellow bell peppers, seeded and cut into thin strips
6 oz	sliced smoked iguana, chopped
1 1/4	cups mozzarella cheese, cut into cubes
2	Tbsp chopped fresh basil
	salt and black pepper

Preheat the oven to 425 degrees. Place the pizza crusts well apart on two greased baking pans. Brush the pizza crusts with 1 tablespoon of the oil, then brush generously with tomato paste.

Stir-fry the peppers in half the remaining oil for 3-4 minutes. Arrange the iguana and peppers on top of the sun-dried tomato paste. Sprinkle on the mozzarella and basil. Season to taste with salt and black pepper.

Drizzle on the remaining oil and bake in the oven for 15-20 minutes, until crispy and golden. Serve immediately.

Louisiana Rice

4 Tbsp	vegetable oil
1	small eggplant, diced
8	ounces of ground iguana
1	green bell pepper, seeded and chopped
2	stalks of celery, chopped
1	onion, chopped
1	clove garlic, crushed
1 tsp	cayenne pepper
1 tsp	paprika
1 tsp	black pepper
1/2 tsp	salt
1 tsp	dried thyme
1/2 tsp	dried oregano
2 cups	homemade or canned chicken stock
3/4 cup	long-grained rice
8	ounces iguana livers, minced
1	bay leaf
3 Tbsp	chopped fresh parsley
	celery leaves, to garnish

Heat the oil in a frying pan until really hot, then add the diced eggplant and stir-fry for about 5 minutes. Add the iguana and cook for about 6-8 minutes until browned using a wooden spoon to break up any lumps Add the chopped green pepper, celery, onion, garlic, and all the spices and herbs. Cover and cook over high heat for 5-6 minutes, stirring frequently from the bottom up and distribute the crispy brown bits. Pour on the chicken stock and the stir to clean the bottom of the pan. Cover and cook for 6 minutes over medium heat.

Stir in the iguana livers, cook 2 minutes then stir in the rice and add the bay leaf.
Reduce the heat and simmer for about 6-7 minutes. Turn off the heat and let stand for another 10-15 minutes, until the rice is tender. Remove the bay leaf and stir in the chopped parsley. Serve the rice garnished with celery leaves.

If you have stories, recipes or comments you would like to see included in the next edition of this book, email me at TheIguanaHunter@yahoo.com

Many people come to Florida from all over the world each year. Accidents do happen, so if you are moving here or just visiting, please take the time to learn about our amazing and diverse native wildlife. Take the steps that you may need to take to keep your children, pets and yourself SAFE. You can find more information online at MyFlorida.com.

Most of this information was taken from Wikipedia, a free online encyclopedia.